For my dad

Thank you: Dapo Adeola, Anna K. Dalton, Vanessa Davis, Rita Fürstenau, Tom Gauld, Vic Helwani, Karl Kerschl, and Candace Wu.

SIMON & SCHUSTER BOOKS FOR YOUNG READERS

An imprint of Simon & Schuster Children's Publishing Division

1230 Avenue of the Americas, New York, New York 10020

© 2022 by Matthew Forsythe

Book design by Jonathan Yamakami © 2022 by Simon & Schuster, Inc.

SIMON & SCHUSTER BOOKS FOR YOUNG READERS

and related marks are trademarks of Simon & Schuster, Inc.

For information about special discounts for bulk purchases, please contact Simon & Schuster

Special Sales at 1-866-506-1949 or business@simonandschuster.com.

The Simon & Schuster Speakers Bureau can bring authors to your live event.

For more information or to book an event, contact the Simon & Schuster Speakers Bureau

at 1-866-248-3049 or visit our website at www.simonspeakers.com.

The text for this book was set in Goudy Modern MT Std.

The illustrations for this book were rendered in watercolor, gouache, and colored pencil.

Manufactured in China

1121 SCP

First Edition

2 4 6 8 10 9 7 5 3 1

Library of Congress Cataloging-in-Publication Data

Names: Forsythe, Matthew, 1976– author, illustrator.

Title: Mina / Matthew Forsythe.

Description: First edition. | New York : Simon & Schuster Books for Young Readers, [2022] |

"A Paula Wiseman Book." | Audience: Ages 4–8. | Audience: Grades 2–3. | Summary: Mina the mouse is

very upset when her father brings home a pet "squirrel" that she is certain is a cat.

Identifiers: LCCN 2020050689 (print) | LCCN 2020050690 (ebook) |

ISBN 9781481480413 (hardcover) | ISBN 9781481480420 (ebook)

Subjects: CYAC: Mice—Fiction. | Cats—Fiction. | Pets—Fiction. |

Fathers and daughters—Fiction. | Humorous stories.

Classification: LCC PZ7.1.F663 Min 2022 (print) | LCC PZ7.1.F663 (ebook) | DDC [E]—dc23

LC record available at https://lccn.loc.gov/2020050689

LC ebook record available at https://lccn.loc.gov/2020050690

MINA

MATTHEW FORSYTHE

A Paula Wiseman Book
Simon & Schuster Books for Young Readers
New York London Toronto Sydney New Delhi

Mina lived in her own little world
where nothing ever bothered her.

Except for one thing.

It wasn't her father,
who was always bringing
home surprises from
the outside world.

And it wasn't the tin can he found
that made his jokes louder.

And it wasn't the collection of antique art
that he thought would make them rich.

And it wasn't even the band
of musicians he met in the woods.

She barely noticed any of those things.

But one day her father came home
and said, "Mina! Come outside.
I have a really big surprise for you!"

And that's when she started to worry.

"It's a squirrel!" he said.

"I don't think that's a squirrel," said Mina.

"Of course it is. Squirrels are bigger
than mice and have long bushy tails!"

"I don't know," said Mina.

That night Mina couldn't sleep.

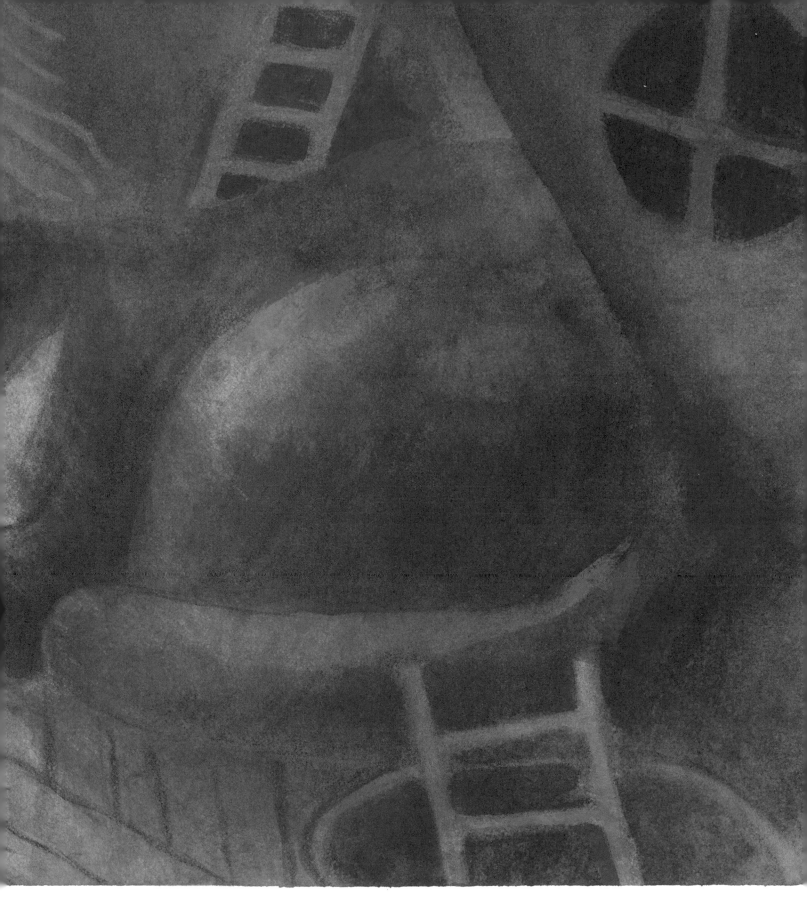

"There's nothing to worry about,"
said her father.

"Remember the time I brought home those
stick insects and you taught them to read.
That was so much fun."

"They stole all my books!" said Mina.
"We got you more books," said her father.

"Now go to sleep.
    Everything will be fine.
    You'll see."

"I don't know," said Mina.

But sure enough everything was fine.

For a little while.

Until one day,

Mina's father said, "He's not eating!
Something's wrong.
Do you think he's lonely?"

"Perhaps," said Mina. "But whatever you do,
don't bring home any more surprises."
But the next day . . .

he brought home
two more surprises.

But they wouldn't
eat either.

So Mina's father
called the doctor,
who came right
away.

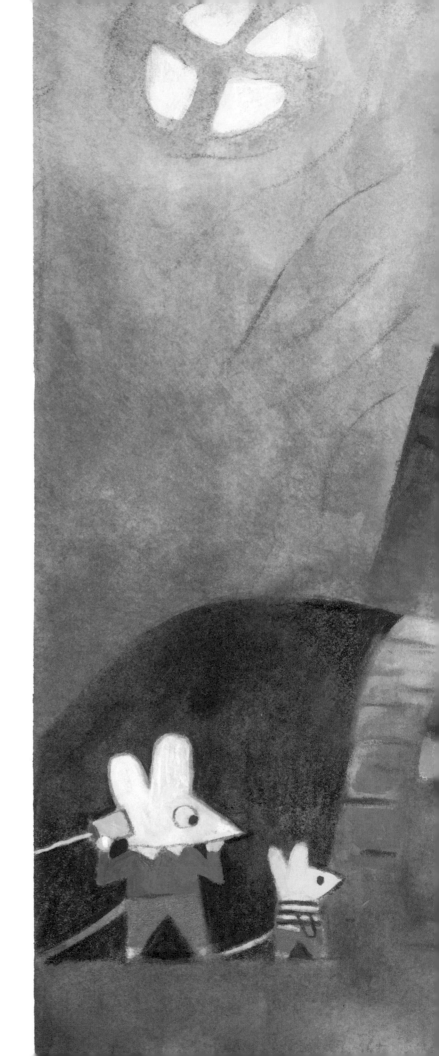

"I'm sure there's nothing to worry about," said the doctor.

"But let me take a look at these squirrels."

"Oh, I see the problem," said the doctor.
"The problem is that these squirrels
are definitely cats."

"Oh no," said Mina's father.
"Oh dear," said Mina.
And then all at once . . .

the cats chased Mina and her father
and the doctor into the woods.

And over the pond.

And up a tree.

When finally Mina said,

"Stop!

"We shared our home with you!
  Our food! Our toothpaste!

"And this is how you repay us?
  By trying to eat us?"

"Yes," said the cats.

And they were about to eat the mice
when the strangest thing happened.

A stick insect walked slowly
into the fray.

And she licked her finger and
opened a book and started reading
out loud with a deep charismatic
voice—which is how all stick
insects sound.

And the cats slowly,

slowly,

fell asleep.

Quietly, Mina and her father
and the doctor stole away.

"I told you everything would
   be fine," whispered Mina's father.

And even though she rolled her
little eyes, Mina had to admit that,
for once,

he was right.